This book belongs to:

_____

The illustrations were created using gouache and colored pencil
The text and display type were set in Stone Informal and Oneleigh
Composed in the United States of America
Designed by Lois A. Rainwater
Edited by Aimee Jackson

NORTHWORD

Books for Young Readers
NorthWord Press
18705 Lake Drive East
Chanhassen, MN 55317
www.northwordpress.com

Library of Congress Cataloging-in-Publication Data

Warrick, Karen Clemens.
Who needs that nose? / by Karen Clemens Warrick ; illustrated by Sherry Neidigh.
p. cm.
Summary: The reader is asked to guess what a creature is from a description of the
appearance and use of its nose. Includes notes on the noses of various animals.
ISBN 1-55971-887-0
[1. Nose—Fiction. 2. Animals—Fiction.] I. Neidigh, Sherry, ill. II. Title.

PZ7.W2576Wh 2004

[E]—dc21   2003048760

My second picture book

for my second grandson—

Baylor Warrick

—K. C. W.

For Dad

—S. N.

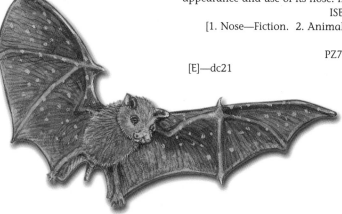

Printed in Singapore
10 9 8 7 6 5 4 3 2 1

Who Needs THAT Nose?

by Karen Clemens Warrick

illustrated by Sherry Neidigh

NorthWord PRESS
Chanhassen, Minnesota

Who needs a nose

that swings and sways,

a long, gray nose that works like a hand

to pick up nuts or bunches of hay?

Who needs that nose?

Elephant

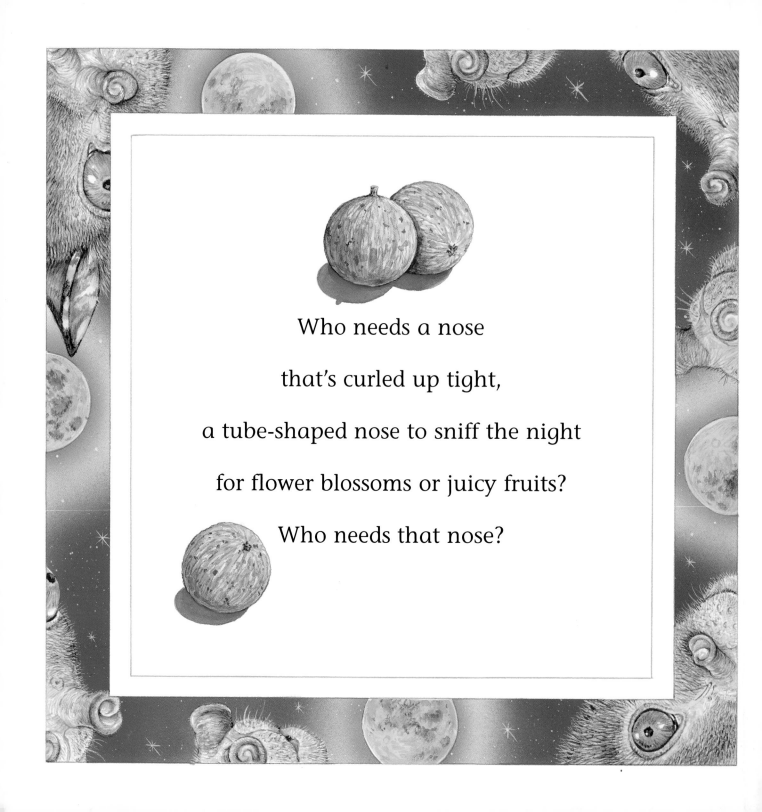

Who needs a nose

that's curled up tight,

a tube-shaped nose to sniff the night

for flower blossoms or juicy fruits?

Who needs that nose?

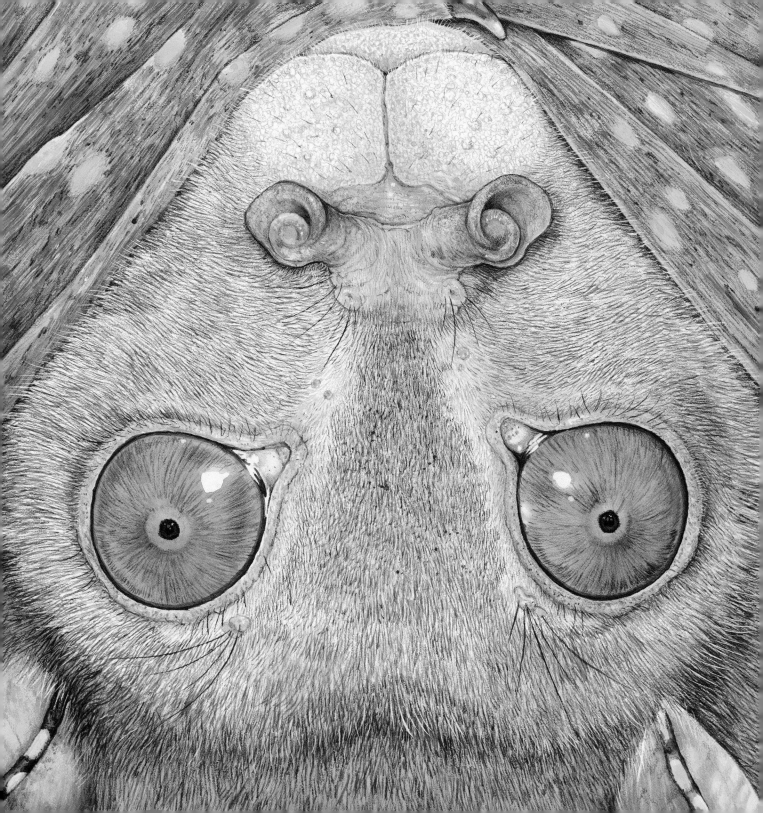

Bat

Who needs a nose

pink as a flower,

a nose with twenty-two little fingers

that wiggle and squirm when

searching for worms?

Who needs that nose?

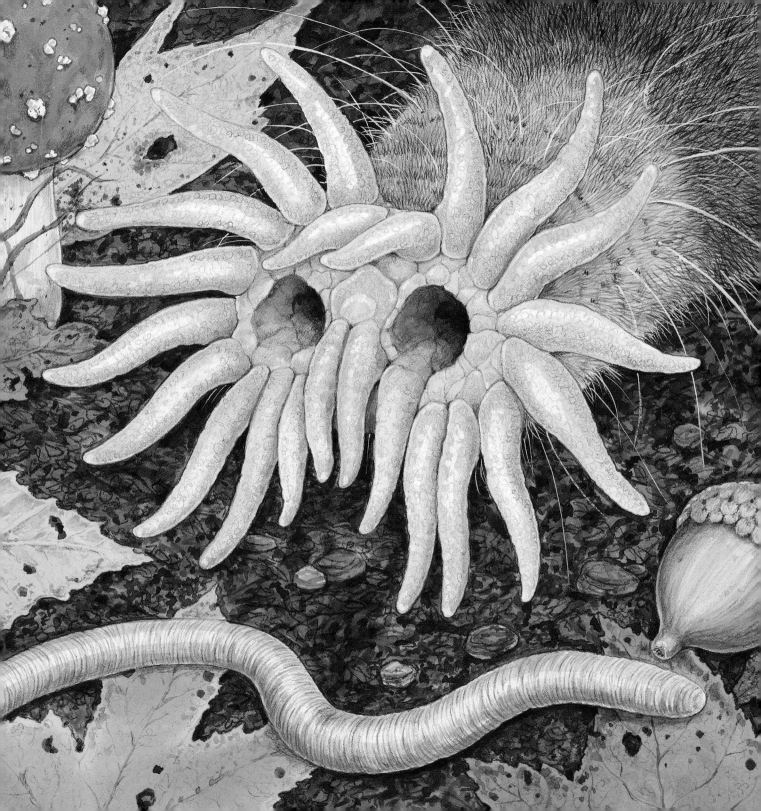

Mole

Who needs a nose

on top of its head,

a nose that shuts tight underwater,

then spouts like a fountain as it breathes out?

Who needs that nose?

Whale

Who needs a nose

to poke around,

a nose that reaches down, down, down

to sniff termites

and ants underground?

Who needs that nose?

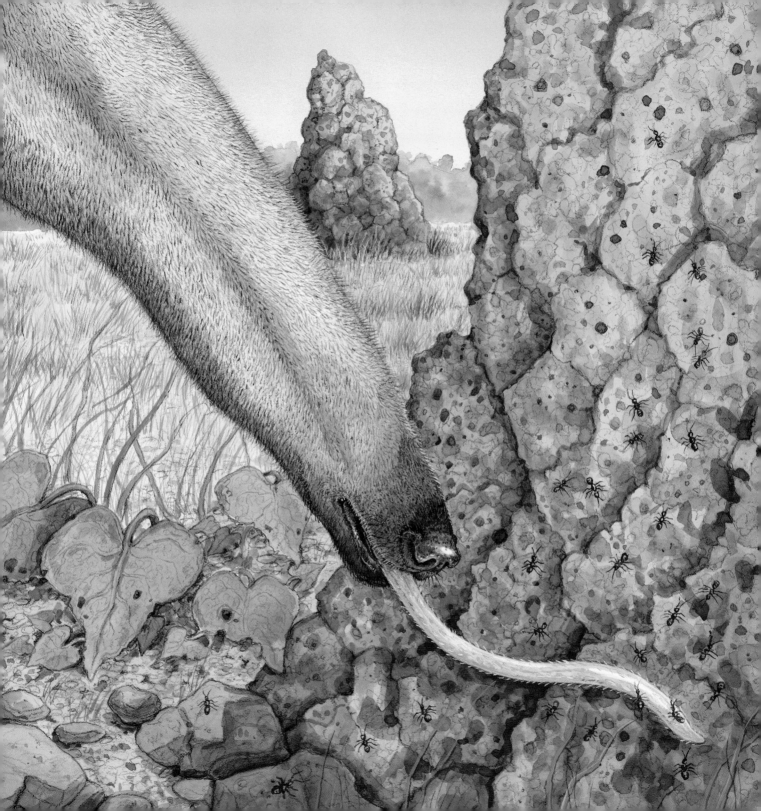

Anteater

Who needs a nose

to attract a mate,

an enormous nose

that droops

down to his chin?

Do you suppose

it hides a grin?

Who needs that nose?

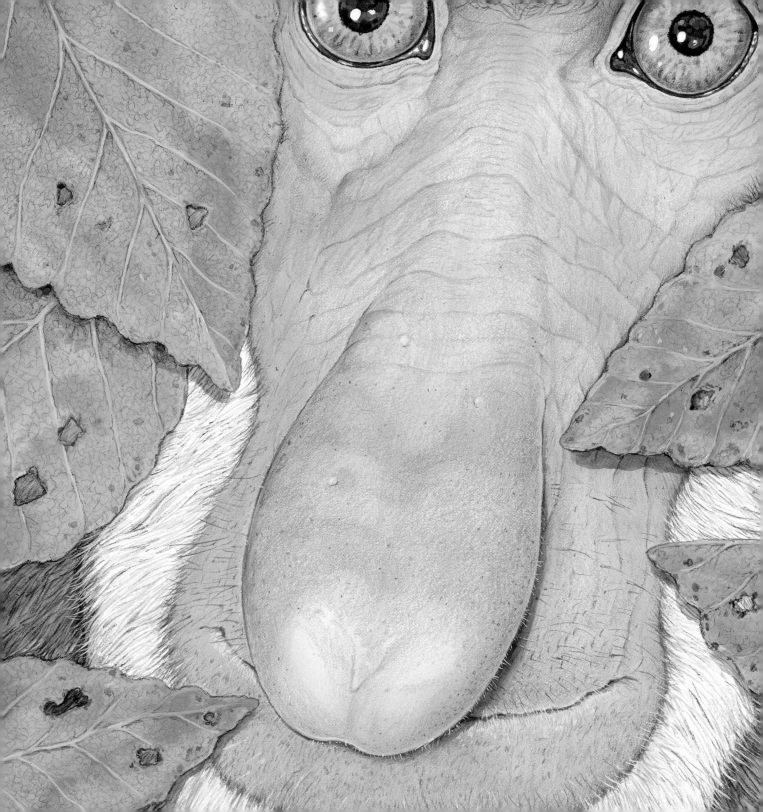

Monkey

Who needs a nose,

to prop sunglasses up,

a nose to smell popcorn

and chocolate chip cookies,

or one that makes

quite a breeze with a sneeze?

Who needs that nose?

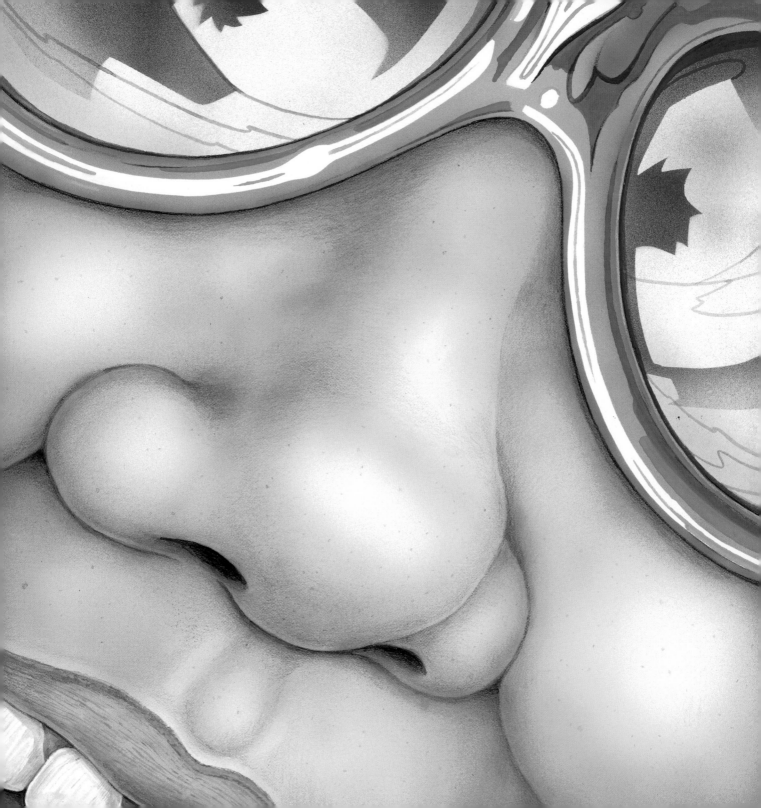

Nosey Notes

A SUPER SNIFFER

African Elephant's trunk is part nose, part upper lip, and part hand. Its trunk tip can pick up small objects the way you use your thumb and forefinger. Elephant can use its trunk to slurp up water and give itself a shower, or to playfully spray others. When Elephant sticks its trunk straight up in the air, it is sniffing for danger.

FLY-BY-NIGHT NOSE

Tube-Nosed Bat may look silly, but it is a super smeller. It uses its rolled up nostrils to sniff its favorite foods. Mother bat depends on her nose to tell her which of the upside-down babies is hers.

A REALLY WEIRD NOSE

Star-Nosed Mole has one of the world's strangest noses. Twenty-two fingers circle its snout. Some people think they look like flower petals. The fingers move quickly back and forth as Mole tunnels underground to search for insects, worms, and grubs.

HOLD THAT NOSE

Humpback Whale's blowhole helps it stay underwater for as long as forty minutes. It gulps in a huge breath, closes its special nose, then dives down to hunt dinner. When Whale comes back to the surface of the water, it opens its blowhole and spouts out water vapor and air at speeds up to 300 miles (483 km) per hour. Some whales have one blowhole. Others have two.

DIG THAT NOSE

Giant Anteater's nose can sniff out its favorite treats, termites and ants, underground. First it uses strong claws to rip open the insects' hill. Then it pokes its long, skinny snout down into the maze of tunnels and slurps up bugs. What a yummy meal!

ANOTHER NAME FOR NOSE

Proboscis Monkey's nose is weird and marvelous. It uses its nose to breathe and smell. Also, Monkey's nose gets bigger and turns red when it is looking for a mate. Sometimes an oversized nose is called a "proboscis."

YOUR NOSE

Your nose has some pretty important jobs, too. It helps you breathe air in and out. It can smell good things you like to eat. It also helps keep you safe. If your nose smells smoke, you might be in danger. Dust and dirt can tickle your nose. Then you sneeze. Just for fun, you can wiggle your nose, or scrunch it up to make a funny face.

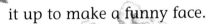

Who Needs That Nose? is KAREN CLEMENS WARRICK'S second picture book for young children. She has also written educational books for teachers and biographies and histories for middle-grade students. Writing is Karen's second career. Before she became an author, she taught school for fifteen years. Now she enjoys visiting classrooms as a guest author. She lives with her husband, Jim, and their three dogs in Prescott, Arizona. To learn more about the author, visit her Web site: www.karenclemenswarrick.com.

SHERRY NEIDIGH has been a freelance illustrator for sixteen years and has illustrated numerous children's books, including *If I Had a Tail* by Karen Clemens Warrick. Sherry collects nutcrackers and vintage toys from the 1960s. One of her favorite animals to draw and also collect is the duckbill platypus because of its unusual features. Sherry currently lives in Charlotte, North Carolina, with her two sheltie dogs, Basil Knawbone and Chloe.